ana & ANDREW

A Snowy Day

by Christine Platt
illustrated by Sharon Sordo

Calico Kid

An Imprint of Magic Wagon
abdobooks.com

About the Author
Christine A. Platt is a historian and author of African and African-American fiction and fantasy. Christine enjoys writing stories for people of all ages. She currently serves as the Managing Director of The Antiracist Research and Policy Center at American University.

For Nalah, Gabby and our fun-filled snowy days. —CP

For Leo, For believing in me from the beginning. —SS

abdobooks.com

Published by Magic Wagon, a division of ABDO, PO Box 398166, Minneapolis, Minnesota 55439. Copyright © 2019 by Abdo Consulting Group, Inc. International copyrights reserved in all countries. No part of this book may be reproduced in any form without written permission from the publisher. Calico Kid™ is a trademark and logo of Magic Wagon.

Printed in the United States of America, North Mankato, Minnesota.
102018
012019

Written by Christine Platt
Illustrated by Sharon Sordo
Edited by Tamara L. Britton
Art Directed by Candice Keimig

Library of Congress Control Number: 2018947940

Publisher's Cataloging-in-Publication Data

Names: Platt, Christine, author. | Sordo, Sharon, illustrator.
Title: A snowy day / by Christine Platt; illustrated by Sharon Sordo.
Description: Minneapolis, Minnesota : Magic Wagon, 2019. | Series: Ana & Andrew
Summary: It's the season's first snowfall! School is canceled, and Ana & Andrew play in the snow with their neighbors and learn to make snow ice cream. They save some snow cream in the freezer for their cousins in Trinidad who have never seen snow.
Identifiers: ISBN 9781532133534 (lib. bdg.) | ISBN 9781644942574 (pbk.) |
  ISBN 9781532134135 (ebook) | ISBN 9781532134432 (Read-to-me ebook)
Subjects: LCSH: Snow--Juvenile fiction. | Ice cream, ices, etc--Juvenile fiction. | Cousins--Juvenile fiction. | Snowballs--Juvenile fiction.
Classification: DDC [E]--dc23

Table of Contents

Chapter #1
Where's the Snow?

Ana and Andrew stood at the living room window and looked up at the sky. Ana's favorite doll, Sissy, sat on the window ledge and looked outside too.

"Are you sure it's going to snow?" Ana asked.

Mama walked over and stood next to Andrew. "It's definitely cold enough. I do believe we will soon see this winter's first snow."

"I sure hope so," Andrew said.

Winter was one of Ana and Andrew's favorite seasons. They loved to play in the snow. And afterward, Mama always made hot chocolate with marshmallows to warm them up. The news had forecast snow but not one snowflake had fallen from the sky.

Ana and Andrew kept waiting. Soon, the sun was setting. After dinner, they peeked out the window one last time.

"It's still not snowing," Ana said sadly. She hugged Sissy.

"Maybe it will snow tomorrow." Mama kissed Ana on the cheek. "Right now, it's time for bed."

Ana and Andrew put on their favorite pajamas. Ana's pajamas were covered with pictures of books because she loved to read. Andrew's pajamas were covered with pictures of airplanes.

After Ana and Andrew were dressed, they brushed their teeth. Then, Papa tucked them into bed and read them a story about a happy snowman, which made Ana and Andrew laugh.

"Good night," Ana said to Andrew. Then she whispered to Sissy, "Good night."

"Good night," Andrew replied. "I am going to dream about snow."

"Me too," Ana said.

Then they closed their eyes and went to sleep.

Chapter #2
Snow Surprise!

The next morning, Mama came into their room. "Good morning," she sang, as she always did.

"Good morning, Mama," Ana and Andrew said.

"I think you should look outside." Mama smiled.

Ana and Andrew ran to their window and pulled back the curtains.

"Look!" Ana shouted.

Andrew did a wiggle-dance.

"Snow!"

Large white snowflakes were falling from the sky. Their entire neighborhood was covered in snow, even Papa's car.

"Surprise!" Mama laughed.

After breakfast, Mama helped them get dressed. First, Ana and Andrew put on their pants and long-sleeved shirts. Next, they put on their warmest socks. Then they put on their snowsuits and boots.

Every winter, Grandma knit hats, scarves, and mittens for Ana and Andrew. She even made a tiny matching hat and scarf for Sissy. Ana smiled as Mama helped them put on the last of their winter gear.

"Are you ready?" Papa asked.

"Yes!" Ana and Andrew said excitedly.

Mama opened the front door. Ana and Andrew ran outside to play in the snow.

Chapter #3
Snow Cream

Ana and Andrew's neighbors and friends were playing in the snow.

Ana went next door to visit Chloe. "Would you like to play with me and Sissy?"

"Yes!" Chloe and Ana took turns helping Sissy walk in the snow. Then Papa came outside and helped them build a snowman.

Andrew walked to Robert's house. His other friends, Mike and John, were there too. "Hi Andrew," they said.

"Hi!" Andrew watched Robert, Mike, and John place some bowls on the ground. "What are you guys doing?"

"We are catching fresh snow so we can make snow cream," Robert explained.

"What's snow cream?" Andrew asked.

"It's like ice cream," John said. "Only better because you make it with snow."

"Wow!" Andrew had never heard of snow cream.

"Would you like to help us make some?" Mike asked.

"Yes!" Andrew said excitedly. He put two bowls in the snow—one for him and one for Ana. Once the bowls were filled with snow, Robert's mother gave them sugar and milk to mix with the snow.

"Time for snow cream!" Robert shouted.

"Ana, come try your snow cream," Andrew called out to his sister.

"On the count of three,
everyone takes a bite," John said
as everyone dipped their spoons
in the snow cream. "One, two,
three!"

"It tastes delicious!" Ana let Sissy
taste a little. "And Sissy thinks so
too. Thank you!"

Everyone enjoyed their snow cream
on the first snowy day of winter.

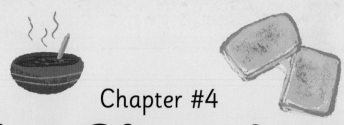

Chapter #4

Hot Chocolate & Hugs

At noon, Ana and Andrew went inside for lunch. Mama made grilled cheese sandwiches and tomato soup. Ana and Andrew dipped their sandwiches in their soup because they thought it tasted best that way.

"Did you enjoy playing in the snow?"
Mama asked.

"Oh yes," Ana said. "Chloe and I took Sissy for a walk. Then Papa helped us build a snowman. It looked just like the happy snowman in the story we read yesterday."

"And then, we ate . . ." Andrew looked at Ana and smiled.

"Snow cream!" they shouted together.

"Oh my," Papa said. "What a treat!"

"I wish our cousins could taste snow cream," Ana said. "I know they would love it."

Ana and Andrew's cousins lived on the island of Trinidad. It was always hot there, so there were never any snowy days.

"Maybe you can make snow cream and freeze it," Mama suggested. "Then they can taste it when they come visit us this summer."

"Yes!" Ana clapped her hands. "We can surprise them like they surprised us!"

The last time Ana and Andrew visited their family in Trinidad, their cousins surprised them with sugar cake from their end of school party.

Ana and Andrew loved the sugary sweet treat, especially because it was made with bits of coconut! It was fun to try Caribbean food because it was so different than the food they normally ate.

"That's a great idea!" Papa said.

"Let's do it," Andrew said.

"But I have something special for you first." Mama handed them a cup of hot chocolate. There were a lot of marshmallows floating at the top. Andrew did a wiggle-dance, and everyone laughed.

"I just love snowy days," Ana said.

"We all do." Papa smiled.

"Group hug!" Andrew opened his arms wide and hugged everyone in his family. "Today was a perfect snowy day."